Alligator Arrived with Apples

A Potluck Alphabet Feast

by Crescent Dragonwagon

pictures by Jose Aruego & Ariane Dewey

Aladdin Books
Macmillan Publishing Company • New York   Maxwell Macmillan Canada • Toronto
Maxwell Macmillan International • New York Oxford Singapore Sydney

First Aladdin Books edition 1992 • Text copyright © 1987 by Crescent Dragonwagon • Illustrations copyright © 1987 by Jose Aruego and Ariane Dewey • All rights reserved. No part of this book may be reproduced or transmitted in any form or by any means, electronic or mechanical, including photocopying, recording, or by any information storage and retrieval system, without permission in writing from the Publisher.
Aladdin Books, Macmillan Publishing Company, 866 Third Avenue, New York, NY 10022 • Maxwell Macmillan Canada, Inc., 1200 Eglinton Avenue East, Suite 200, Don Mills, Ontario M3C 3N1 Macmillan Publishing Company is part of the Maxwell Communication Group of Companies. **Printed in Hong Kong** 10 9 8 7 6 5 4 3 2 1
The text of this book is set in 18 point ITC Zapf International italic. The illustrations are rendered in pen-and-ink and gouache. A hardcover edition of Alligator Arrived with Apples *is available from Macmillan Children's Books.*

Library of Congress Cataloging-in-Publication Data • Dragonwagon, Crescent. Alligator arrived with apples : a potluck alphabet feast / by Crescent Dragonwagon; pictures by Jose Aruego & Ariane Dewey. p. cm. Summary: From Alligator's apples to Zebra's zucchini, a multitude of alphabetical animals and foods celebrate Thanksgiving with a grand feast. ISBN 0-689-71613-3 [1. Alphabet. 2. Animals—Fiction. 3. Thanksgiving Day—Fiction.] I. Aruego, Jose, ill. II. Dewey, Ariane, ill. III. Title. PZ7.D7824Ak 1992 [E]—dc20 91-38490

Amanda C,
the very least
an aunt can do
is have a feast

With cakes and pies
in gooey pieces
and relatives,
especially nieces!

We'll have the family
A to Z
but first of all,
Amanda C!
                    —C.D.

To Juan
        —J.A. and A.D.

A *feast for you*
A *feast for me*
A *feast that goes from A to Z!*

A feast for us
and several guests
A feasting full Thanksgiving fest!

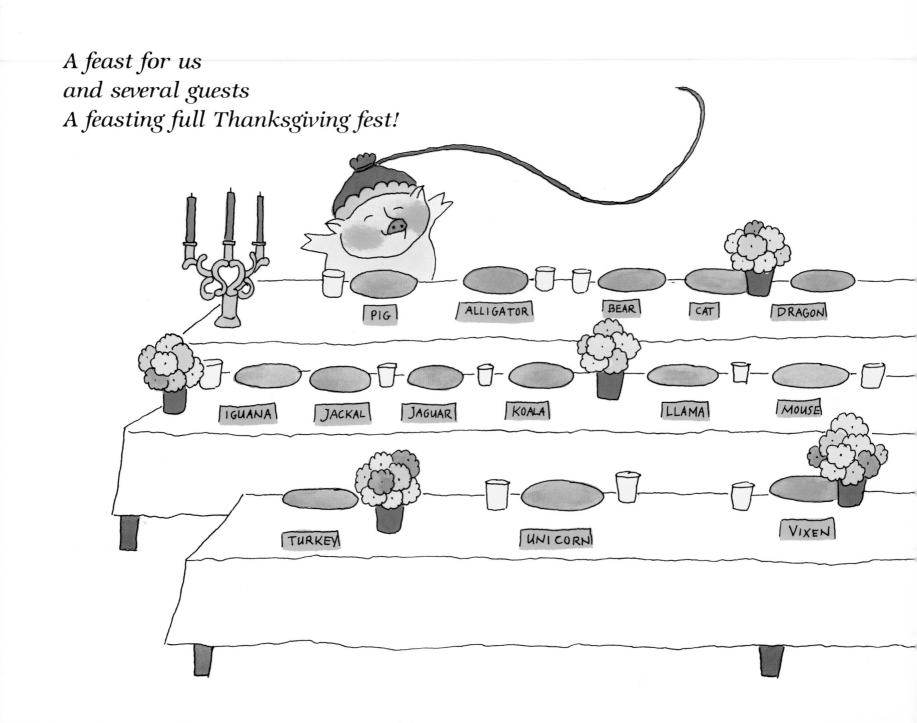

The table's full
Our friends are here
We'll eat from now until next year!

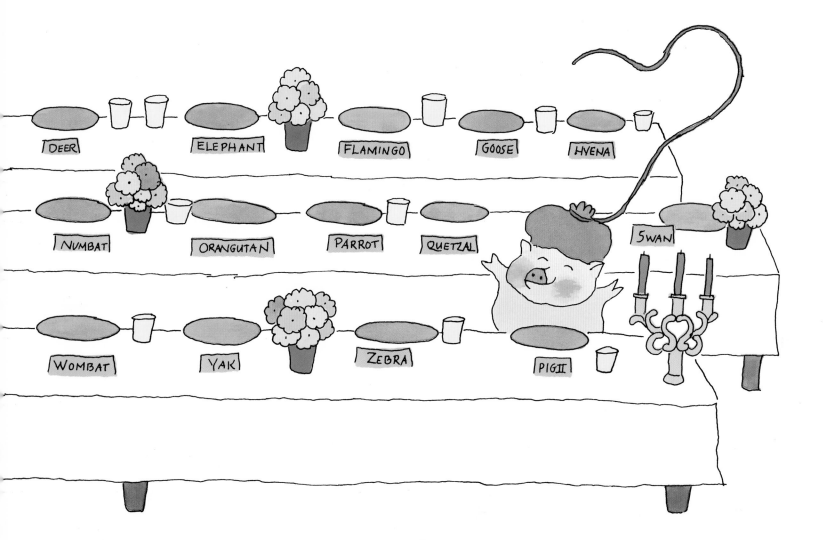

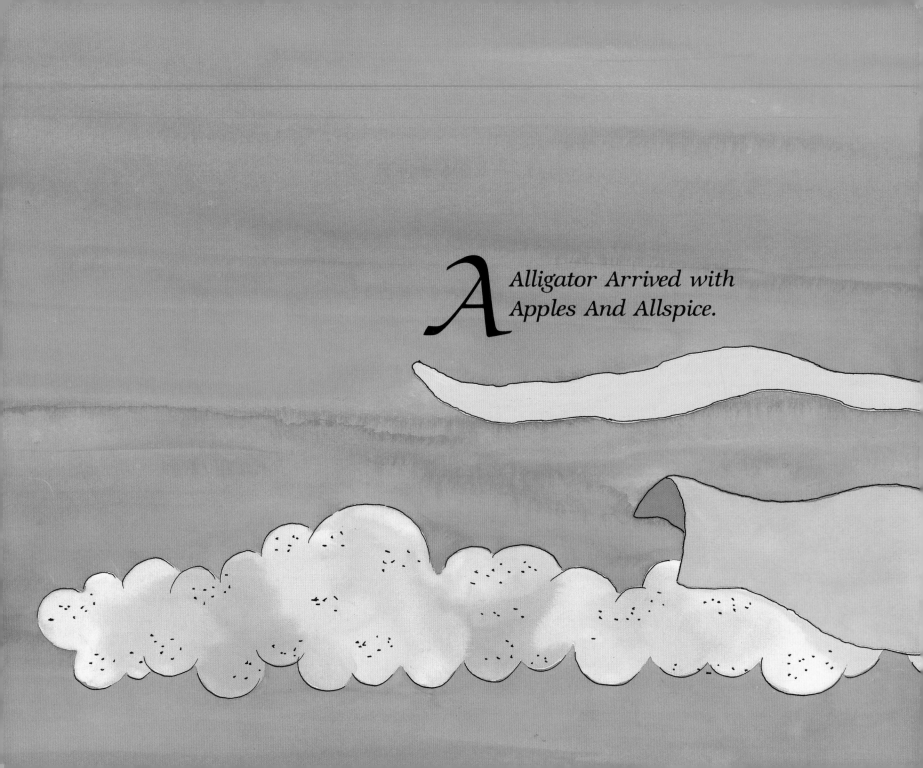

Alligator Arrived with
Apples And Allspice.

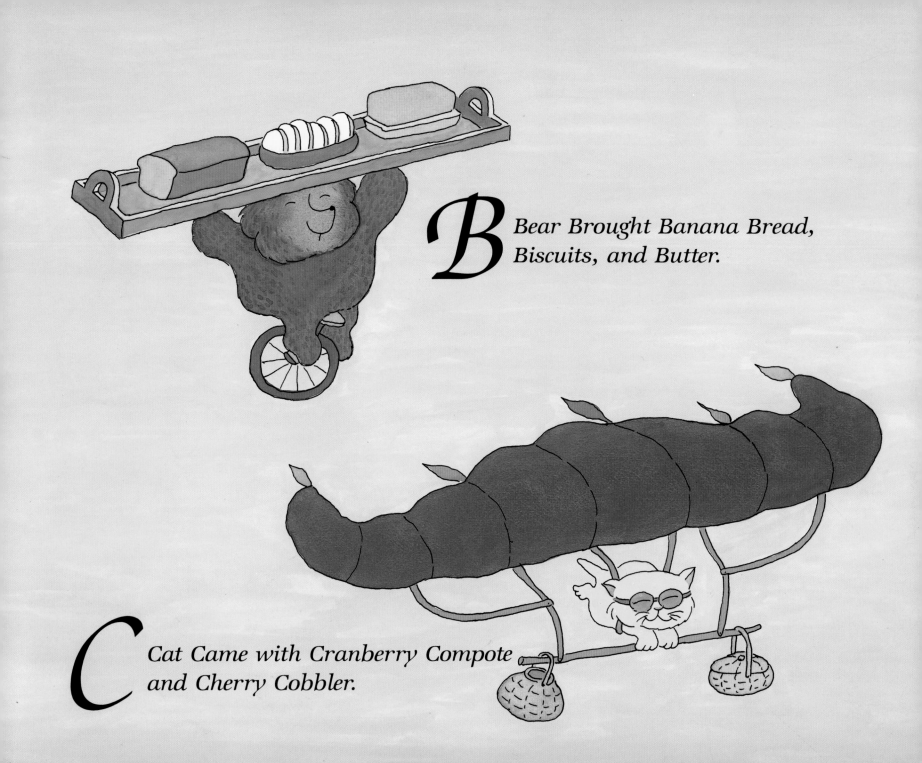

B Bear Brought Banana Bread,
Biscuits, and Butter.

C Cat Came with Cranberry Compote
and Cherry Cobbler.

*D*ragon and Deer Diced Dates
and Delivered them to the Door.

E Elephant Eclipsed Everyone with his Elderberry Elixir.

F Flamingo Found Fabulously Flavored Fresh Figs and Fixed them Flambé.

G Goose Gave Gravy, Grapes, and Gingerbread.

H Hyena Had the Hiccups, but He Hailed us with Honey and Hazelnuts.

I Indira of India Imparted Ice cream.

J Joe from Jerusalem
Juggled Juices,
Jams, and Jellies
with Jaguar.

K Koala Kicked in Kale, Kohlrabi, and Kasha.

L Llama Lugged Lemons, Limes, and Lingonberries.

M There was Mocha Mousse
Made by Mouse,

N Noodles from Nick of Naples,

O and Onions and Olives
Offered by Orangutan.

P Pumpkin Pie and Pickled Peaches
were Provided by Parrot,

Q and there were Quinces from the Queen,
R as well as the Royal Red Relish.

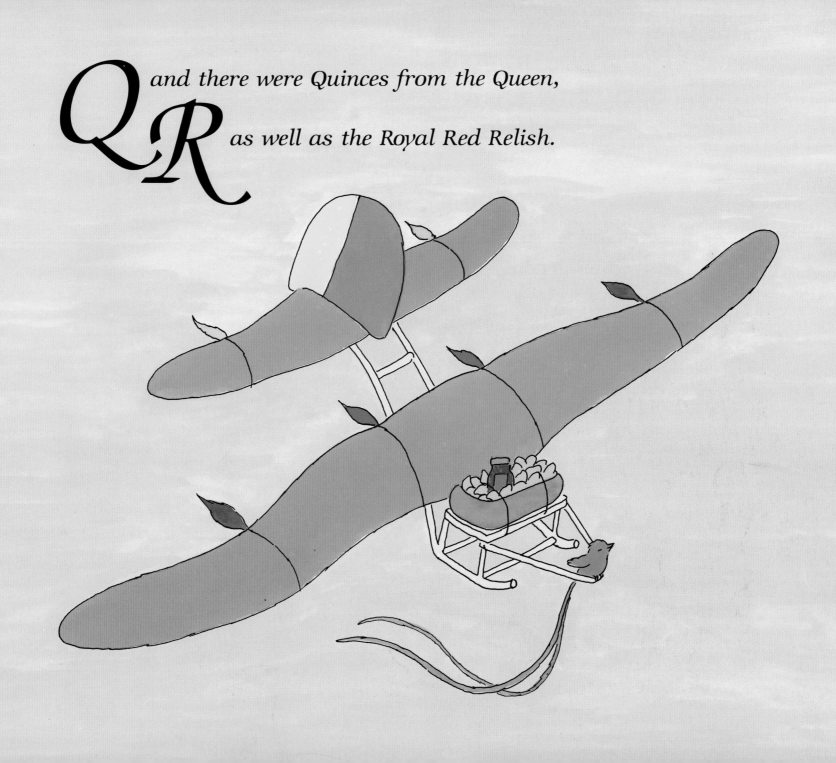

S Swan Served Sage Stuffing and Squash Soufflé.

T Turkey Turned up with Tomatoes, Trifle, and Turnips.

U Avoiding Unpleasantness
with the Use of an Umbrella,
Uncle Umberto Unwrapped
Upside-down cake.

V Vixen Violated tradition
with Valentines.

*W*ombat *W*hipped up
*W*ild rice and *W*alnuts *W*ith *W*ine,

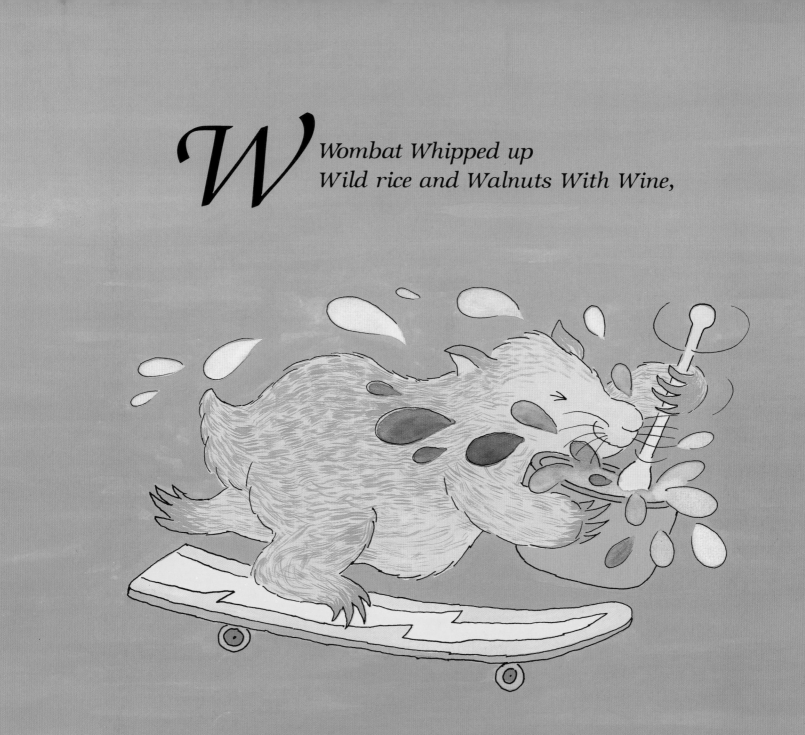

and e *X*cellent

*Y*ams and Yogurt
were Yielded by Yak.

*Z*ebra Zipped over
a Zaftig Zucchini.

We ate our way
from A to Z
Enough for you? Too much for me!

We ate so much
There are no scraps
It's time for our Thanksgiving naps!

Our sleep is deep
And many snore
When we wake up
we'll eat some more!

O thanks for friends
For food, for cheer
I'm glad Thanksgiving's once a year!